Moon Phases

As the Moon circles the Earth, the amount of light that the Moon reflects from the Sun changes how the Moon looks in the sky. It takes about 29.5 days for the Moon to circle the Earth which means the Full Moon happens about once a month.

Full Moons

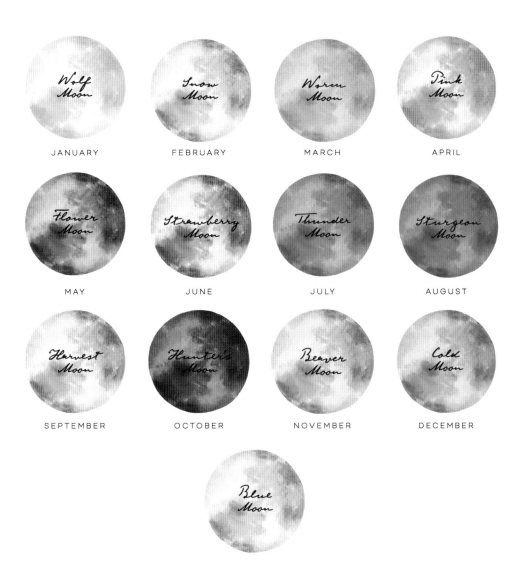

Wolf Moon	Snow Moon	Worm Moon	Pink Moon
JANUARY	FEBRUARY	MARCH	APRIL
Flower Moon	Strawberry Moon	Thunder Moon	Sturgeon Moon
MAY	JUNE	JULY	AUGUST
Harvest Moon	Hunter's Moon	Beaver Moon	Cold Moon
SEPTEMBER	OCTOBER	NOVEMBER	DECEMBER

Blue Moon

Once in a Blue Moon: A Blue Moon usually occurs once every two to three years. Whenever there are two full moons in a month the second full moon is the Blue Moon.

For Ben and Luci

Created by: Karly Bonfante
Illustrated by: Kenzie Raposo
Contributing writer: Talia Sand

First Printing, 2024

Library of Congress Control Number: 2023917422 | ISBN: 979-8-9890587-0-9

For the full series and more Full Moon Fairy magic please visit us at
www.fullmoonfairy.com.

Adding more
magic to the
magic years.

CONNECT WITH US
fullmoonfairy.com | hello@fullmoonfairy.com

Full Moon Fairy

FAYE & FRIENDS

by Karly Bonfante

Hello!
My name is Faye,
Fairy of Moonlight
Big Sister to Cute Critters
and the Brightener of Night.

Like our gang of nighttime creatures, you may simply call me Faye.

Quick now, my newest friend,
It's time for the soiree!

Darkfall sometimes calls for an extra festive celebration

When it happens on the eve of the
night sky's new rotation.

When the moon blooms all rounded,
like a bursting red ripe berry.

It's a merry grand affair
for any friend or full moon fairy.

When everyone who's nocturnal
(meaning creatures up all night)

Turns their eyes up toward the sky,
it's really quite a sight.

Whether fur, fins, scales, or feathers,
we will always flock together,

How long has this been happening?
Perhaps it's been forever.

We'll drum up a simple ditty full of
chirps, purrs, howls, and growls

Harmonized from up high with a few
hoots from the owls.

And the tides, indeed
they'll rise, and the reefs
way down below?

You would not believe it,
friend, but by moonlight,
they will grow.

Not only does the full moon look
so magically enchanting,

It also douses grounds, so they're all
prepared for planting.

Now the timing is quite ripe to give some
brand-new life a chance,

Little squiggly wiggly earthworms slither up to
slide and dance.

Now listen up my Moon Friends,
if you're still not a believer:
There's this charming breed of bird called
a white-browed sparrow-weaver.

The boy bird chirps a tune, to enchant a Juliet
And before you even know it, their song's
a sweet duet.

Full moons bring new gifts -
I think about it a whole lot,

Should I send something to you?
A little trinket, or whatnot?

Somewhere hidden from the moolight,
that's exactly where I'll choose.

Oh, I think I've got it!
I will place it in your shoes.

Lay them out,
I'll find them and leave behind a thoughtful treat

I will promise not to mind,
if they smell like stinky feet.

You might find yourself surprised
if you forget you've heeded my warning,
And your toes wiggle with tickles
when you get dressed in the morning.

I hope that you will like them,
all the gifts that I've selected,

Just some little somethings that are meant
to help us learn and stay connected.

Things to keep Earth feeling clean
and the air all nice and airy,

A big ask kind of task
for any kid or kind of fairy.

Now we've got you and we've got me, and all things beneath the moon. Together we are ready for the new starts coming soon.

When the full
moon sort of
swoons and the
stars all start to spark,
Even the blackest of
nights will stop feeling
quite as dark.

Oh, the fun we will get up to
when that last day's sun goes down.
And the lightning bugs, they'll start to buzz,
and brighten up your town.

After all, we're all connected,
if you just look to the light,

You might find a full moon waiting,
now I bid you a good night!

A final wish from me to you,

May each rustle of leaves sing tales of magic and every dew-kissed petal unfold secrets just for you. May the night sky be your canvas, painted with constellations of endless possibilities. With a heart open to the symphony of nature, may you discover the magic hidden in every corner of this world.

Before I go, don't forget to leave your shoes out for me on the eve of the next full moon! Under the luminous moonlight, they shall become a bridge between your world and mine.

Till we meet again,

Faye ♡

Cathedral Caverns State Park, which has roughly 50,000 visitors per year, four full-time employees, and six part-time workers a year, has been awarded a 2016 Certificate of Excellence by Trip Advisor. In addition to the cave tour, the park has both camping and backcountry camping. A local jewel, the cave has become something of a family tradition. Possessing vivid memories of their first visit, parents and grandparents hope to share those experiences with future generations. Cathedral Caverns remains a shining member of the Alabama State Park System. Jay Gurley would be extremely proud! After all, he always maintained that his primary goal was to share the cave with the world. He did just that and more. The history of Cathedral Caverns is, at its core, the story of Jay Gurley. (Author's collection.)

DISCOVER THOUSANDS OF LOCAL HISTORY BOOKS
FEATURING MILLIONS OF VINTAGE IMAGES

Arcadia Publishing, the leading local history publisher in the United States, is committed to making history accessible and meaningful through publishing books that celebrate and preserve the heritage of America's people and places.

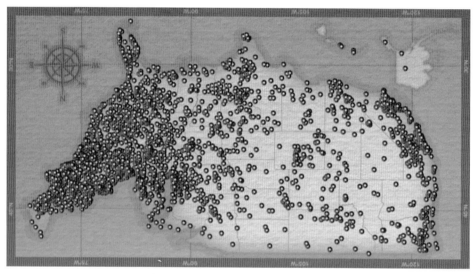

Find more books like this at
www.arcadiapublishing.com

Search for your hometown history, your old stomping grounds, and even your favorite sports team.